To Madeleine, Mimi, and Josh,
with love, from your sister who adores you!
—A. R.

To Amy, with love and true respect
—A. B.

ATHENEUM BOOKS FOR YOUNG READERS
An imprint of Simon & Schuster Children's Publishing Division
1230 Avenue of the Americas, New York, New York 10020
Text copyright © 2012 by Amy Reichert
Illustrations copyright © 2012 by Alexandra Boiger
ATHENEUM BOOKS FOR YOUNG READERS is a registered trademark
of Simon & Schuster, Inc.
For information about special discounts for bulk purchases, please
contact Simon & Schuster Special Sales at 1-866-506-1949 or
business@simonandschuster.com.
The Simon & Schuster Speakers Bureau can bring authors to your
live event. For more information or to book an event, contact the
Simon & Schuster Speakers Bureau at 1-866-248-3049 or visit our
website at www.simonspeakers.com.
Book design by Ann Bobco
The text for this book is set in Clarendon LT Std.
The illustrations for this book are rendered in pencil, colored
pencil, black tea, a wee bit of watercolor, and the computer.
Manufactured in China
0112 SCP
First Edition
10 9 8 7 6 5 4 3 2 1
Library of Congress Cataloging-in-Publication Data
Reichert, Amy.
Take your mama to work today / Amy Reichert ; illustrated by
Alexandra Boiger. — 1st ed.
p. cm.
Summary: Violet is very helpful when she visits her mother's
office, and gives pointers on delivering the mail (be sure to
decorate it with extra stamps and stickers), helping the boss with
his big presentation (like a show-and-tell for grown-ups), and
making business cards (after clearing the paper jam in the copier).
ISBN 978-1-4169-7095-8 (hardcover)
[1. Offices—Fiction. 2. Work—Fiction. 3. Mothers and daughters—
Fiction. 4. Humorous stories.] I. Boiger, Alexandra, ill. II. Title.
PZ7.R2637Tak 2012
[E]—dc22
2011006649

take your mama to work today

by
AMY REICHERT

pictures by
ALEXANDRA BOIGER

Atheneum
Books for Young Readers
New York London Toronto Sydney

Snow days.

Half days.

Babysitter's sick today?

Take Your Child to Work Day!

You never know
when you might
have to go to work
at the office.

So be prepared.

As soon as you enter the office building, it's important to . . .

hop

across the entire lobby floor
on just the black squares

all the way to the elevator and push
the **UP** button. Grown-ups love it
when kids push elevator buttons for them.

When you get to your floor,
an excited crowd will be there
to greet you.

They'll say,
"You are *so* cute!"
and
"You have grown *so* big!"

And someone just like Mrs. Honey
will show you her secret candy
drawer and whisper,

"You can take as
much as you want,
whenever
you want it."

Don't be surprised by all the fuss.

Grown-ups love it when
kids visit the office—
they'll treat you just like
a movie star!

Sometimes the boss won't say hello because he'll be getting ready for a presentation— that's like **show-and-tell** for grown-ups. You're probably an expert at show-and-tell, so be sure to offer to help.

If the boss says he's

"too busy,"

don't worry about it.

This is a perfect time to get started
on all the important work you have to do.
First, you'll need a few supplies.

Sharpen your pencils

and put them in your desk, or in a pencil cup, or line them up, or spell your name with them. Putting one behind your ear lets people know you are serious about your job. As soon as you make a name tag, you are officially ready to work.

When the telephone rings, tap the red flashing
button with the eraser end of your pencil
and answer in your most grown-up voice.

"Hello,
Ms. Whimsey's office,
please hold."

Here's an important tip to keep in mind—

"Hello?
Is anyone there?"

DO NOT HANG UP

THE PHONE BEFORE YOU PUSH THE HOLD BUTTON FIRST!!!

Snack time

at the office is called a "coffee break."
Feel free to skip the coffee and take
extra doughnuts instead.

And remember, you can visit

with your colleagues—

that's what **friends**

at the office are called.

But be sure to stick to
office-appropriate topics—
like the traffic and weather
and someone's goofy-
looking new baby.

When you've had enough,
it's back to work again!

Interviewing someone looking for a job
is a lot like making a new friend.

You can help by asking a few good questions like,
"Do you have any pets?" and "How old are you?"

Sometimes when you do that, your mom will suddenly need you to take a package down to the mailroom

"Right away!"

and

"Urgently!"

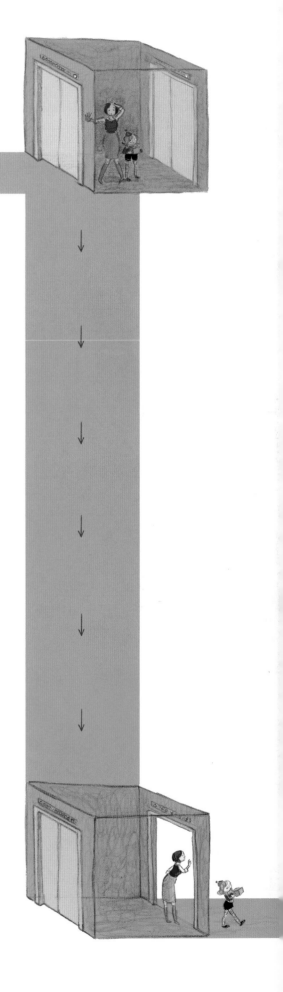

You can be a huge help in the mailroom, too.

The mail people will
be so happy with
your work,

they'll probably send you back
upstairs for an early lunch break.

If the office is having
a power lunch in the conference
room—that's like a really
boring picnic—
feel free to liven things up with
a quick game of chair tag.

Sometimes when you do that,
your mom will suddenly
need you to go keep an
eye on her fish.

This is a good time to make
yourself a business card.
Now's the time to brag—
list absolutely everything
you can do!

Find a nice adult to teach
you how to use the copy
machine, and teach *them*
how to add a snazzy
personal touch.

Here's another important tip—

DO NOT PUSH

1

AND

1

AND

1

IF YOU WANT

THREE

COPIES!!!

Another nice adult might try to show
you how to use the hole punch
and the paper shredder.

They probably don't know you're already

a confetti-making expert!

If by now you're all worn out,
don't worry about it.
Luckily, they do nap time
at the office too!

After your nap, you might want to check in on the boss again. Even bosses get nervous before show-and-tell, so let him know you can help. And this time, don't take no for an answer.

First, tell him to practice.

Then say, "Great job!" when he's done. It's important to feel confident when you do show-and-tell.

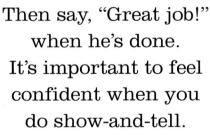

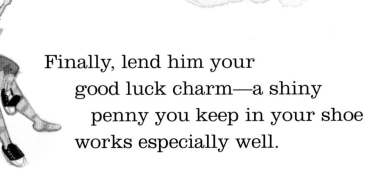

Finally, lend him your good luck charm—a shiny penny you keep in your shoe works especially well.

When the boss gives his presentation, sit in the
back and give him a thumbs-up. And when he's done,
stand and clap really loudly. It's good to set
a positive example.

"I couldn't have done it
without
Violet's help!"

Take this opportunity to
hand out your extra business cards—
that's what grown-ups call "networking"!

Now your work is done. It's time to go home. Everyone will be sad to see you leave. But you can remind them you are only a phone call away.

And promise to come back again really soon—maybe even next week!!

Then push the DOWN button to call the elevator,

and the L button inside the elevator,

and . . .

hop, hop, hop, hop

across the entire lobby floor,

on the white squares only,

right out the door.